Don't Bully Phil Bully

Andre Hillery

NEWMAN SPRINGS PUBLISHING
320 Broad Street
Red Bank, NJ 07701

First originally published by Newman Springs Publishing 2024

ISBN 978-1-63881-105-3 (Paperback)
ISBN 978-1-63881-106-0 (Digital)

Printed in the United States of America

To Daniel Briggs
RIP

Don't Bully Phil Bully

Once upon a time,
there was a Bully
named Phil,
who lived in a town
that was known
for making steel.
Phil was raised
by his dad named Bill
and his mother, Cecil.
Where
the Bully family stayed
was always real chill.
It was one
of the nicest houses
on top of a hill.
Phil's dad, Bill,
owned the Old Mill
where local town workers made the still.
Bill woke up early
way before Phil
and was gone by 7:30
to be at the Old Mill.

Phil's mom, Cecil,
always start her day
with Bill's lunch ready,
and there was no delay.
She made breakfast for Phil before he went to school.
Cecil
loves being Phil's mom
and Bill's wife too.
Phil went to school
with kids just like him.
They walked.
They talked.
They laughed.
They grinned.
They would always
tell Phil
they would be his friend.
But don't bully Bully
are that's the end.
When recess came,
Phil was never next
at the tetherball pole
because
Phil played the best.
He played with
Michael,
John,
Jordan,
and Gian.
These were four
of Phil's best friends.
Jordan told Phil,
"If you are my friend,

don't bully Bully
and go to the end
of the tetherball line because you always win."
Now recess was over
and it was back to class.
Michael said,
"Phil,
that 10 minutes was fast.
In the tetherball game,
you ended up last."
Phil paid it no mind
and worked;
they had a bunch
their teacher
wanted them to finish
all work before lunch.
Gian
whispered to Phil,
"Man,
be on my team.
We get to play kickball when the lunch bell rings."
It was time for lunch
and the kids were excited.
They turned in their work and out the door
they glided.
Gian yelled,
"Phil,
he's on my team."
Michael was like,
"Gian,
what do you mean?"
John said,
"Phil,

if you are my friend,
don't bully Bully
are that's the end."
The kickball game was fun, and Phil played the best.
So Gian's team won
and Jordan was upset.
Michael asked Phil
to borrow a pin.
to finish his work
from when lunch begins.
"Thanks, Phil,"
said Michael.
"You are my friend.
But don't bully Bully,
our that's the end."
They went back to class
and had two hours left
Before school was out
to go home and rest.
Finally,
finally,
the school bell rang.
Gian was so happy
he started to sing.
(La-la-la)
The Old Mill was by
the school they attended.
They raced
to the building
after school ended.
John said,
"Hey,
I know this turf.

Phil,
Isn't this where
your dad works?"
Phil looked in the window, and he saw his dad.
His eyes start to water because Phil was sad.
It was a long day
of being picked on
by friends.
Telling Phil
don't bully Bully
our that's the end.
"Why do they tell me
don't bully Bully?
Do they not know
this makes me feel funny?"
When Phil got home,
his mom
was doing chores.
She was
straightening the couch
after
sweeping the floors.
"How was school, Phil?"
Cecil asked her son.
Phil said,
"Mom,
I'm glad the day's done."
"Is everything okay?"
Cecil asked Phil.
Phil said,
"Mom,
I'm just
a little ill."

Phil's mom could tell
that something was up.
But she didn't want
to press Phil
for what.
When Phil's dad got home,
it was 5:30.
Phil's mom,
Cecil,
had dinner ready early.
They sat down for supper and Bill said grace.
Then he asked Phil
how was his day.
Phil said,
"Today
wasn't all that great.
The guys
picked on me
every time we played."
Bill said,
"I understand.
I saw the look on your face
when you
passed the Old Mill.
I wanted to say hey.
But work was busy
With 100
steel orders
in different
colors,
sizes,
shapes,
and quarters."

Cecil said,
"That's good, Bill,
more work for the people."
Phil was just quietly
eating his Jell-O.
After supper was over,
Phil cleared the table.
His dad
went to relax
and watch a little cable.
Phil's mom,
Cecil,
said,
"Boys will be boys.
Don't worry about it, Phil. They were just making noise.
Just making noise
Phil was thinking.
It was more serious
like
which soda
he's drinking.
Phil went to his room;
he had homework to do.
He had no math,
just science
and
English too.
He finished
all his math
when Phil was at school.
He loved
playing with numbers, charts,
and graphs too.

Phil wanted to be
an engineer one day
in arrow dynamics
to design lots of planes.
Phil had big plans
and he set goals.
By watching his dad, Bill,
at the Old Mill
that Bill owned.
Phil finished his homework
then Phil had to stop.
It was 8:30
almost 9 o'clock.
Phil said,
"Oh no
I have to get some sleep."
He put on his pajamas
then Phil brushed his teeth.
He said
good night
to his mom
and
good night
to his dad.
He dove in his covers
and Phil went to bed.
The next day at school,
Phil was real distant.
"I need to find
some new friends,"
to himself
Phil mentioned.
When first recess came,

Phil stayed in class.
Michael
asked John,
"What's up with that?
Phil loves to be first
at the tetherball pole."
Gian said,
"Where is Phil?"
Jordan said,
"I don't know."
Gian said,
"Without Phil,
it's just not the same."
Michael said,
"Phil's a bully,
and he always complains."
First recess
was over;
the boys
went back to class.
Phil
was at the chalkboard working on math.
Gian said,
"What's up, Phil?"
Phil said, "Hey."
Michael said,
"Move, Phil,
you're in my way."
John and Jordan
was in the back of the class.
They heard what Michael said to Phil
and they started to laugh.
Phil went to his desk

and started his work.
Thinking to himself,
These guys are jerks.
Phil was trying not
to get his feelings hurt.
10 minutes to go
and it was time for lunch.
Gian had some candy
he was waiting to crunch.
The bell rang for lunch
and the boys did not heist.
Gian said,
"Phil,
want some candy?"
Phil said,
"No thanks."
The boys played kickball
but Phil disappeared.
He went
to play basketball
so he didn't hear.
"Don't bully Bully
our that's the end."
Phil started thinking,
Those aren't my friends.
Gian is cool,
but
Michael
John and Jordan
always act like
I'm not important.
The bell rang to end lunch
and it was back to class.

Gian came in first
and Phil came in last.
Phil sat in front of Gian
so they could kind of talk.
Phil asked Gian,
"Did you have fun
at lunch?"
Gian said,
"Not really.
Someone was missing.
But I understand
why you've been distant.
The guys
have been jerks,
saying bully don't Bully.
I don't even laugh
because to me
it's not funny.
Now, Phil,
let's please be quiet
before we get in trouble.
You know how
the teacher gets
as soon as we huddle."
Last recess
finally came
and Phil
left class first,
telling himself,
"I'm going back
to the courts."
Phil played
a game of 21

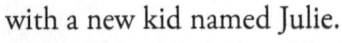

with a new kid named Julie.
Never once did she say "don't bully Bully."
They played one on one
and Julie was good.
She beat Phil
by 3 points.
He played
hard as he could.
Julie said,
"I had fun, Phil."
Phil said,
"Me too.
Can I walk you to class,
Julie?"
Julie said,
"Phil, that's cool."
Phil was so happy:
no Michael
no John
no Jordan.
When Phil got to his class, his work needed sorted.
It was
the last hour of school
and all the kids were silent.
They had a test to take
from
yesterday's assignment.
When the school bell rang,
they turned in their test.
Gian yelled,
"Hold up, Phil."
Phil was like,
"What's next?"

Gian asked
if he was walking
by the Old Mill.
Phil said,
"Not today.
My dad's
off work early
and outside the school gate."
Gian said,
"Okay, Phil,
I'll see you tomorrow."
Phil said,
"Gian, your ears
please let me borrow.
Me and you are cool
I consider you
my friend.
But
Michael,
John,
and Jordan.
bullied me
till
THE END."

About the Author

Picture Taken By Shoua Hang

Andre Hillery was born and raised in the inner cities of Northern California. Coming from a single-parent home, he was highly influenced by the environment that surrounded him. He saw and dealt with bullying not only in school but also in the neighborhood where he lived. Andre's motivation to write a book on bullying comes from a YouTube video that he saw about a mother who lost her son due to the heinous act of bullying. This video brought Andre to tears for two days. Andre would watch this video over and over and over again, thinking to himself, *I have to do something to help stop the heinous acts of bullying across the world*—and that is the reason why Andre dedicates this book to Daniel Briggs.

RIP, Daniel Briggs. Even though you're gone, we will make sure that you are not forgotten, and we are making it our sole mission to eradicate the heinous act of bullying.